1.本書的使用方法

STEP-1

請先找個看起來和藹可親、面容慈祥的英國人，然後開口向對方說：

> 對不起！打擾一下！
> **Excuse me.**

STEP-2

出示下列這一行字請對方過目，並請對方指出下列三個選項，回答是否願意協助「指談」。

> 這是指談的會話書，方便的話，是否能請您使用本書和我對談？
> **Do you have time to communicate with me by this conversational book?**

➡

> 好的！沒問題
> **OK, no problem.**
>
> 不太方便！
> **No, it's inconvenient to me.**
>
> 我沒時間
> **Sorry, I have no time for this.**

STEP-3

如果對方答應的話（也就是指著 "OK, no problem."）請馬上出示下列圖文，並使用本書開始進行對話。
若對方拒絕的話，請另外尋找願意協助指談的對象。

> 非常感謝！現在讓我們開始吧！
> **Thank you so much! Shall we go on?**

2.版面介紹

① 本書收錄有十個單元三十個主題,並以色塊的方式做出索引列於書之二側,讓使用者能夠依顏色快速找到所需要的內容。

草莓派
Strawberry pie

巧克力
chocolate

② 每一個單元皆有不同的問句,搭配不同的回答單字,讓使用者與協助者可以用手指的方式溝通與交談,全書約有超過150個會話例句與2000個可供使用的常用單字。

藥房
Pharmacy
P.80

書店
Bookstore
P.53

③ 在單字與例句的欄框內,所出現的頁碼是與此單字或是例句相關的單元,可以方便快速查詢使用。

④ 當你看到左側出現的符號與空格時,是為了方便使用者與協助者進行筆談溝通或是做為標註記錄之用。

Please

★在希斯洛機場出境...
工具為HEARTHR...
倫敦市中心則所需...

⑤ 在最下方處,有一註解說明與此單元相關之旅遊資訊,方便使用者參考。

形容詞
Adjective.

我是
I am

你是
You

⑥ 最後一個單元為常用字詞,放置了最常被使用的字詞,供使用者參考使用。　　　　　P.84

附錄
Appendix

formation

我住在
I live in the

⑦ 隨書附有通訊錄的記錄欄,讓使用者可以方便記錄同行者之資料,以利日後連絡。　　P.92

護照(要影...
簽證(有的國...
飛機票(要影...
重要度
現金(零錢也...
信用卡

⑧ 隨書附有<旅行攜帶物品備忘錄>,讓使用者可以提醒自己出國所需之物品。　　　　　P.93

英國
B R I T A I N

蘇格蘭
SCOTLAND

北愛爾蘭
NORTHERN
IRELAND

都伯林
Dublin

愛爾蘭
IRELAND

威爾斯
WALES

英格蘭
ENGLAND

倫敦London

3.常用的問候語

　　英語的問候語大都是一些慣用語，因此最好的學習方法就是反反覆覆的多念幾次，直到能朗朗上口為止，至於何謂「朗朗上口」呢？簡單的說就是當你想向人道謝時，結果在第一時間衝口而出的居然是「Thank you.」而不是「謝謝！」，那麼你就算「學成」！

　　以下的各句問候用語，你不妨每句先念個一百次，你馬上就可以體驗到何謂「 英語朗朗上口」的快樂滋味，不信的話就請試試看吧！

早安 Good morning.	你好嗎？ How are you?
晚安 Good evening.	晚安（臨睡前的問候語） Good night.

麻煩你 Sorry to bother you.	謝謝 Thank you.	
沒關係 Never mind.	對不起 Sorry.	再見 Good-bye.
不好意思（詢問、叫人、引人注意時的用語） Excuse me.		

稱呼 Title		先生 Sir	小姐 Miss
女士 Madam	朋友 Friend	同伴 Pal	同學 Classmate

＊經常需要用到的句子

我的英文不好。 My English is poor.	
請講慢一點。 Please speak slowly.	
請再說一次。 I beg your pardon.	
請把它寫下來。 Please write it down.	

c o n t e n t s

單元二 從機場到旅館

1.機場詢問

請問您 Excuse me.	謝謝 Thank you.	在哪裡 Where?

入境 Arrival	出境 Departure	觀光 Sightseeing →P.13
是的 yes	不 no	休假出遊 on vacation →P.13
出差 Business tour		留學 Studying abroad

停留多久 How long will you stay? →P.66	過境 Transit
一個禮拜 one week / 二個禮拜 two weeks / 一個月 one month / 一年 one year	

一個禮拜 one week	二個禮拜 two weeks	一個月 one month	一年 one year

★由台灣直飛倫敦的航空公司有長榮及英亞航，而轉機的航空班機則有國泰、新加坡、荷蘭、泰國等。

請問這附近有沒有~~？ Is there any ~~ around here?		洗手間 Rest room
兌幣處 Currency exchange →P.62		免稅商店 Duty-free shop
詢問處 Information	海關 Custom	公車站 Bus station →P.16
計程車招呼站 Taxi stop →P.18	地鐵 Underground →P.16	吸菸區 Smoking area

請問~~在哪裡？
Excuse me, where is the ~~?
→P.14

有前往市區的機場巴士嗎？
Is there any bus to the downtown area?

要在哪裡搭車？
Where should I take the bus?

請幫幫我！
Please help me.

★在希斯洛機場入境者，可以利用地下鐵皮卡地里線至市區，時間約為45分鐘，另一種較為快速的交通工具為HEARTHROW EXPRESS、AIRBUS HEARTHROW SHUTTLE，若是搭乘計程車的話，到達倫敦市中心所需費用可能會超過30英鎊。

2.今晚打算住哪裡？

請問還有房間嗎？
Is there any vacancy?

我在台灣就已經預約了旅館。
I have already made the reservation in Taiwan.

我要住~~天。
I am going to stay for~~days.　→P.62、66

請問住宿費一晚多少錢？
How much for one night?　→P.62

這有包括稅金和服務費嗎？
Is tax and tips included?

有沒有更便宜的房間？
Is there any room for a lower price?

請給我比較安靜的房間。
Please give me a quiet room.

單人房 **Single room.**	
雙人房 **Twin room.**	
飯店 **Hotel**	
便宜的飯店 **Low-priced hotel.**	
旅館 **Inn.**	

現在就可以Check in嗎？
May I check in now?

退房時間是幾點？　→P.66
When should I check out?

這裡的地址？
What's the address here?

這裡的電話號碼?
What's the phone number here?

~在哪裡？ **Where is~~?**	請告訴我~ **Please tell me~~**	客滿 **No vacancy**	櫃台 **Front desk**
緊急出口 **Emergency**	餐廳 **Restaurant**	電梯 **Lift**	廁所 **Rest room**

★ 可查詢住宿資訊的網站有：http://www.accom.co.uk/、http://www.travel-uk.com/tuk/travel-uk-data.htm、
http://www.milford.co.uk/。

我要再多住一天。
I want to stay for one more night.

請幫我換房間。
Please change a new room for me.

這個房間太吵了。
This room is too noisy.

房間裡沒有肥皂
There is no soap in my room.

	毛巾 Towel
	牙刷 Toothbrush
	牙膏 Toothpaste

這個鎖壞了。
The lock is broken.

浴缸的塞子塞不緊。
The bathtub is leaking.

我（不小心）把鑰匙忘在房間裡了。
I forgot my key in the room.

沒有熱水。
No hot water.

電視不能看。
The television is broken.

廁所沒辦法沖水。
I can't flush the toilet.

請叫一個服務生來。
Please send me a waiter.

這個壞了。
This is not working.

空調的聲音太吵，睡不著。
The air conditioner is too noisy, I can't sleep.

房間太冷了。
The air conditioning is too cold.

請再給我一個枕頭。
Please give me one more pillow.

單元三 旅行觀光

單元三 旅行觀光

倫敦全區圖

自助旅行

搭乘電車

搭乘計程車

倫敦精華遊

懶人旅行法

倫敦地鐵圖

單元三 旅行觀光

1.倫敦全區圖

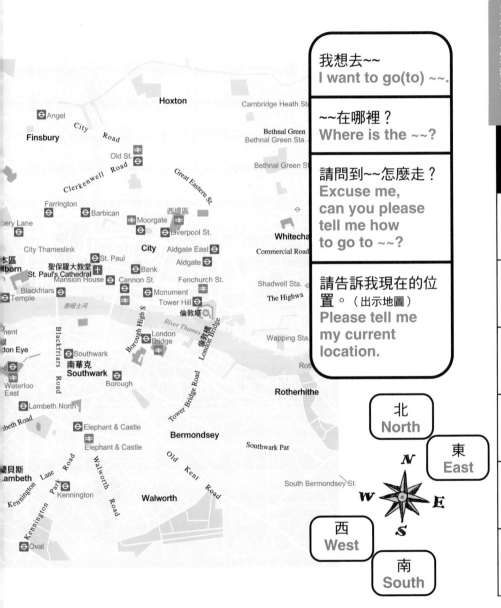

我想去~~
I want to go(to) ~~.

~~在哪裡？
Where is the ~~?

請問到~~怎麼走？
Excuse me,
can you please
tell me how
to go to ~~?

請告訴我現在的位置。（出示地圖）
Please tell me
my current
location.

北
North

東
East

西
West

南
South

單元三 旅行觀光

倫敦全區圖

自助旅行

搭乘電車

搭乘計程車

倫敦精華遊

懶人旅行法

倫敦地鐵圖

2.自助旅行

倫敦全區圖

自助旅行

搭乘電車

搭乘計程車

倫敦精華遊

懶人旅行法

倫敦地鐵圖

我想去~~ I want to go…	~~在哪裡？ Where is …?
請問到~~怎麼走？ Excuse me, how do I go to …?	
這附近有~~嗎？ Is there any … around here?	

洗手間 Rest room	兌幣處 →P.62 Currency exchange
詢問處 Information	警察局 Police station
→P.16 公車站牌 Bus stop	計程車招呼站 →P.18 Taxi stop
→P.50 購物中心 Shopping mall	郵局 Post office
→P.62 銀行 Bank	博物館（美術館） Museum

走路／坐車要多久？ How long does it take by bus / walking?
請問這裡是哪裡？ Excuse me, where is here?
這是什麼路？ What's the name of the road?
請告訴我現在的位置。（出示地圖） Please tell me my current location.

北方 North	東方 East	西方 West	南方 South
前面 Front	後面 Back	上面 Up	下面 Down
直走 Go straight		左轉 Turn left	右轉 Turn right
對面 In the opposite side		紅綠燈 Traffic light	
過馬路 Cross the road			

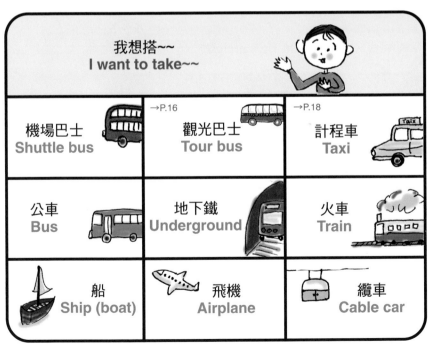

我想搭~~
I want to take~~

機場巴士 Shuttle bus	觀光巴士 Tour bus →P.16	計程車 Taxi →P.18
公車 Bus	地下鐵 Underground	火車 Train
船 Ship (boat)	飛機 Airplane	纜車 Cable car

倫敦全區圖

自助旅行

搭乘電車

搭乘計程車

倫敦精華遊

懶人旅行法

倫敦地鐵圖

15

倫敦全區圖

自助旅行

搭乘電車

搭乘計程車

倫敦精華遊

懶人旅行法

倫敦地鐵圖

3.搭乘電車

到~~的票在哪裡買？
Where can I buy the ticket to ~~?

請問到~~的公車(火車)要到哪裡搭？
Where can I take the bus (train) to ~~?

請給我~~張票。
Please give me ~~ ticket(s).

→P.62

多少錢？
How much?

→P.62

要花多少時間？
How long does it take?

→P.66

下一班車幾點到？
When will the next bus arrive?

→P.66

車票 **Ticket**	公車地鐵月票（週票） **Monthly (weekly) pass**
單程票 **One-way ticket**	日乘車券 **One-day pass**
來回票 **Round-trip ticket**	回數券 **Commutation ticket**

★倫敦市區的地下鐵是全世界最古老的系統，稱為UNDERGROUND或是TUBE，主要有十二條路線，在車站的畫分上分為六個區，只要不出地鐵站，轉車均為免費。

這附近有沒有廁所呢？
Is there any rest room around here?

廁所在哪裡？
Where is the rest room?

我可以借用一下廁所嗎？
May I use the rest room?

單元三 旅行觀光

倫敦全區圖

自助旅行

搭乘電車

搭乘計程車

倫敦精華遊

懶人旅行法

倫敦地鐵圖

搭乘電車 Take a train.	往~~的車是在哪一號月台？ Which platform is the train to ~~?

這班電車開往~~嗎？
Is this train heading to (for) ~~?

這班電車在~~有停嗎？
Will this train stop at ~~?

出口 Exit	剪票口 Gate
換車處 Transfer lounge	私營鐵路線 Private-run railway
地鐵 Underground	成人／小孩 Adult / Child
退返硬幣 Refund	喚人按鈕 Call

★ 如果想要用另一種方式遊覽倫敦，搭乘巴士倒是不錯的考量，尤其是雙層巴士的上層第一排座位，
更是能觀賞到另一種風貌的倫敦。上車時可直接向司機或是車掌購買車票，要下車直接拉鈴即可。

4.搭乘計程車

計程車招呼站在哪裡？ Where is the taxi stop?	請幫我叫一輛計程車。 Please call me a cab.
還沒到嗎？ Aren't we there yet?	已經過了嗎？ Did we pass it?

到~~的時候請告訴我。
Please inform me when we arrive ~

→P.62

到~~要多少錢呢？ What is the fee (fare) to ~~?	請到~~。 Please go to ~~ 

請到這個地址去。（出示地址）
Please go to this address.

(地址 ADDRESS：   )

請在這裡等一會兒。 Please wait here.	請快點！ Please hurry up.
在那裡停車。 Please stop over there.	請一直走。 Please go straight.
請往右邊轉。 Please turn right.	請往左邊轉。 Please turn left.

★ 在倫敦計程車稱為BLACK CAB，不過近來有愈來愈多的顏色和圖案取代了原有的黑色，一般的計程車是以錶計費，也可以打電話叫車，這時則採取議價的方式。

倫敦全區圖

自助旅行

搭乘電車

搭乘計程車

倫敦精華遊

懶人旅行法

倫敦地鐵圖

1. 蘇活區 Soho

我想去～～ I want to go (to) ～～.	～～在哪裡？ Where is the ～～?

請問到～～怎麼走？
Excuse me, can you please tell me how to go to ～～?

請告訴我現在的位置。（出示地圖）
Please tell me my current location.

蘇活廣場 Soho Square	舊康普頓街 Old Compton St.	皮卡地里圓環 Piccadilly Circus	科芬奇街 Coventry St.
萊斯特廣場 Leicester Square	聖馬丁教堂 St. Martin-in-the-Fields	國家藝廊 National Gallery	特拉法加廣場 Trafalgar Square

單元三 旅行觀光

倫敦全區圖

自助旅行

搭乘電車

搭乘計程車

倫敦精華遊

懶人旅行法

倫敦地鐵圖

倫敦全區圖

自助旅行

搭乘電車

搭乘計程車

倫敦精華遊

懶人旅行法

倫敦地鐵圖

2. 西敏區 westminster

Green Park

Cha

禁衛騎兵團
Horsequards Parade

The Mall

維多利亞女王紀念碑
Queen Victoria Memorial

聖詹姆斯公園
St. James's Park

唐寧街**Downin**

白金漢宮
Buckingham Palace

鳥籠道**Birdcage Walk**

聖瑪格麗特教堂——
St. Margaret's Church

St. James's Park

Victoria St.

西敏寺大教堂
Westminster Ab

Victoria

Pimlico

泰特美術館**Tate Gallery**

20

Cross

泰晤士河Thames

宴廳Banqueting House

minster
●西敏碼頭Westminster Pier

大鵬鐘Big Ben

國會大廈
House of Parliament

我想去~~
I want to go (to) ~~.

~~在哪裡？
Where is the ~~?

請問到~~怎麼走？
Excuse me,
can you please tell me
how to go to ~~?

請告訴我現在的位置。
（出示地圖）
Please tell me
my current location.

維多利亞女王紀念碑 Queen Victoria Memorial	
白金漢宮 Buckingham Palace	
鳥籠道 Birdcage Walk	
聖詹姆斯公園 St. James's Park	
禁衛騎兵團 Horseguards Parade	
唐寧街 Downing St.	
國宴廳 Banqueting House	
泰晤士河 Thames	
聖瑪格麗特教堂 St. Margaret's Church	
西敏碼頭 Westminster Pier	
西敏寺大教堂 Westminster Abbey	
國會大廈 House of Parliament	
泰特美術館 Tate Gallery	大鵬鐘 Big Ben

單元三 旅行觀光

倫敦全區圖

自助旅行

搭乘電車

搭乘計程車

倫敦精華遊

懶人旅行法

倫敦地鐵圖

單元三 旅行觀光

倫敦全區圖

自助旅行

搭乘電車

搭乘計程車

倫敦精華遊

懶人旅行法

倫敦地鐵圖

3. 科芬園 Covent Garden

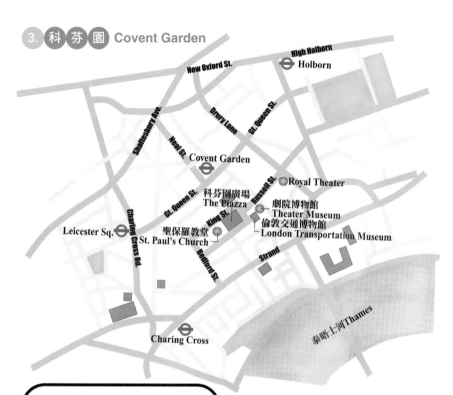

我想去~~ I want to go (to) ~~.		科芬園廣場 The Piazza
~~在哪裡？ Where is the ~~?		聖保羅教堂 St. Paul's Church
請問到~~怎麼走？ Excuse me, can you please tell me how to go to ~~?		劇院博物館 Theater Museum
請告訴我現在的位置。 （出示地圖） Please tell me my current location.		倫敦交通博物館 London Transportation Museum
		泰晤士河 Thames

★ 想要參觀倫敦的眾多博物館，可以考慮購買LONDON WHITE CARD，其時效分為三天和七天二種，可以在有效的時間內參觀倫敦的十六個博物館和藝廊，無次數上的限制。

3. 馬里波恩 Marvlebone

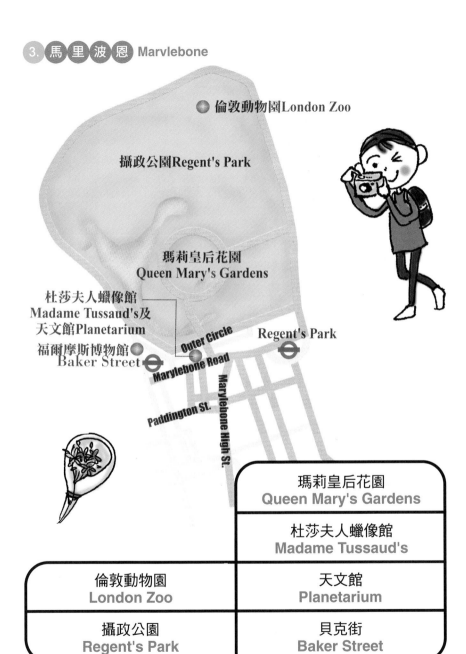

● 倫敦動物園London Zoo

攝政公園Regent's Park

瑪莉皇后花園
Queen Mary's Gardens

杜莎夫人蠟像館
Madame Tussaud's及
天文館Planetarium

福爾摩斯博物館
Baker Street

Outer Circle

Regent's Park

Marylebone Road

Paddington St.

Marylebone High St.

	瑪莉皇后花園 Queen Mary's Gardens	
	杜莎夫人蠟像館 Madame Tussaud's	
倫敦動物園 London Zoo	天文館 Planetarium	
攝政公園 Regent's Park	貝克街 Baker Street	

倫敦全區圖

自助旅行

搭乘電車

搭乘計程車

倫敦精華遊

懶人旅行法

倫敦地鐵圖

單元三 旅行觀光

倫敦全區圖

自助旅行

搭乘電車

搭乘計程車

倫敦精華遊

懶人旅行法

倫敦地鐵圖

5. 肯辛頓 Kensinqton

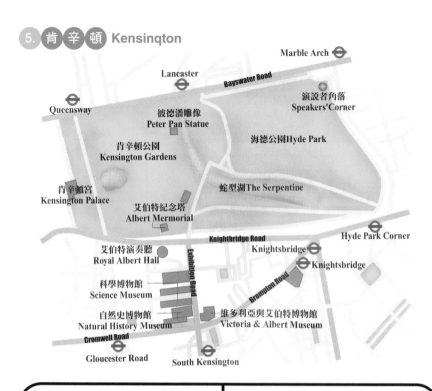

我想去～～ I want to go (to) ～～.	～～在哪裡？ Where is the ～～?
請問到～～怎麼走？ Excuse me, can you please tell me how to go to ～～?	請告訴我現在的位置。（出示地圖） Please tell me my current location.

彼德潘雕像 Peter Pan Statue	演說者角落 Speakers' corner	肯辛頓公園 Kensington Gardens	海德公園 Hyde Park
肯辛頓宮 Kensington Palace	艾伯特紀念塔 Albert Mermorial	蛇型湖 The Serpentine	艾伯特演奏廳 Royal Albert Hall
科學博物館 Science Museum	自然史博物館 Natural History Museum	維多利亞與艾伯特博物館 Victoria&Albert Museum	

6. 西堤區 The City

倫敦全區圖

自助旅行

搭乘電車

搭乘計程車

倫敦精華遊

懶人旅行法

倫敦地鐵圖

我想去~~ I want to go (to) ~~.	~~在哪裡？ Where is the ~~?

請問到~~怎麼走？
Excuse me, can you please tell me how to go to ~~?

請告訴我現在的位置。（出示地圖）
Please tell me my current location.

聖保羅教堂 St. Paul's Church	倫敦塔 Tower of London
英格蘭銀行 Bank of England	泰晤士河 River Thames
皇家交易所 Royal Exchange	聖凱薩琳船塢 St. Katherine's Dock
紀念碑 The Monument	倫敦塔橋 Tower Bridge

25

倫敦全區圖

自助旅行

搭乘電車

搭乘計程車

倫敦精華遊

懶人旅行法

倫敦地鐵圖

7. 南岸區 South Bank

我想去～～ I want to go (to) ～～.	～～在哪裡？ Where is the ～～?
請問到～～怎麼走？ Excuse me, can you please tell me how to go to ～～?	
請告訴我現在的位置。（出示地圖） Please tell me my current location.	

泰特美術新館 Tate Gallery of Modern Art	南華克大教堂 Southwark Cathedral
莎士比亞環球劇場 Shakespeare's Globe	海斯商場 Hay's Galleria

格 拉 斯 哥 Glasgow

我想去~~	~~在哪裡？
I want to go (to) ~~.	Where is the ~~?

請問到~~怎麼走？
Excuse me, can you please tell me how to go to ~~?

請告訴我現在的位置。（出示地圖）
Please tell me my current location.

喬治廣場	人民宮	波勒克之屋
George Square	People's Palace	Pollok House

格拉斯哥大教堂	格拉斯哥現代美術館
Glasgow Cathedral	Glasgow Gallery of Modern

格拉斯哥大學	布萊爾博物館	伊凡尼斯
Glasgow University	Burerell Collection	Inverness

格拉斯哥藝術學院	楊柳茶室	尼斯湖
Glasgow School of Art	The Willow Tea Room	Loch ness

單元三 旅行觀光

倫敦全圖圖

自助旅行

搭乘電車

搭乘計程車

倫敦精華遊

懶人旅行法

倫敦地鐵圖

倫敦全區圖

自助旅行

搭乘電車

搭乘計程車

倫敦精華遊

懶人旅行法

倫敦地鐵圖

愛丁堡城堡 EDINBURGH CASTLE

Georgian House

Castle St.
Charles St.
Queensferry St.
West Maitland St. Shandwick Pl.
Morrison St.
Lothian Rd
King's Stables Rd
Bread St.
West Port
Johnson Terr.
Grassmarket

Queen St.
Frederick St.
David St.
St. Andrew St.
George St.
Princes St.

西王子街花園
蘇格蘭國家畫廊
旅客中心
瓦佛利

愛丁堡城堡
格子呢編織工廠
蘇格蘭威士忌中心
幽靈餐廳
Lawnm
聖吉爾斯
George IV Bridge
Chamber
蘇格蘭國家†

愛丁堡
EDINBURGH

符號說明

博物館	旅客中心	教堂	車站	學院入口	城堡

我想去~~
I want to go (to) ~~.

~~在哪裡？
Where is the ~~?

請問到~~怎麼走？
Excuse me,
can you please tell me
how to go to ~~?

請告訴我現在的位置。
（出示地圖）
Please tell me
my current location.

格子呢編織工廠
Tartan Weaving Mill&Exhibition

蘇格蘭威士忌中心
Scotch Whiskey Heritage Center

幽靈餐廳
Witchery restaurant

單元三 旅行觀光

倫敦全區圖

自助旅行

搭乘電車

搭乘計程車

倫敦精華遊

懶人旅行法

倫敦地鐵圖

PL.

聖瑪麗大教堂

卡爾頓丘陵

Leith St.

North Bridge

Regent St.

Emarket St.

約翰諾克斯之屋

High Street

大家的故事博物館

Canongate

荷里路德宮

兒童博物館

South Bridge

Holyrood Rd.

荷里路德公園

丁堡大學

格雷史東之屋 Gladstone's Land	大家的故事博物館 The People's story Museum
兒童博物館 Museum of Childhood	荷里路德宮 The Palace of Holyroodhouse
王子街 Princes Street	蘇格蘭國家畫廊 The National Gallery of Scotland
國立現代藝術館 The Scottish National Gallery of Modern Art	蘇格蘭國家博物館 The National Museum of Scotland

29

單元三 旅行觀光

倫敦全區圖

自助旅行

搭乘電車

搭乘計程車

倫敦精華遊

懶人旅行法

倫敦地鐵圖

湖 區 Lake District

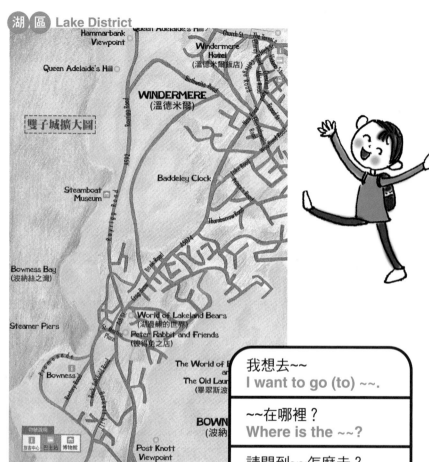

我想去~~
I want to go (to) ~~.

~~在哪裡？
Where is the ~~?

請問到~~怎麼走？
Excuse me,
can you please tell me
how to go to ~~?

請告訴我現在的位置。
（出示地圖）
Please tell me
my current location.

湖區雙子城
Windermere&Bowness

畢翠斯波特的世界
World of beatrix potter

湖邊熊的世界
World of Lakeside Bears

倫敦全區圖

自助旅行

搭乘電車

搭乘計程車

倫敦精華遊

懶人旅行法

倫敦地鐵圖

約克大教堂 York Minster	約克城牆 Ancient York Walls
約維克維京中心 Jorvik Viking Center	石頭街 Stonegate
印象藝廊 Impressions Gallery	克利福德塔 Clifford's Tower
約克城堡博物館 York Castle Museum	約克市立藝廊 York City Art Gallery
約克故事博物館 The York Story Museum	約克郡博物館 Yorkshire Museum

倫敦全區圖

自助旅行

搭乘電車

搭乘計程車

倫敦精華遊

懶人旅行法

倫敦地鐵圖

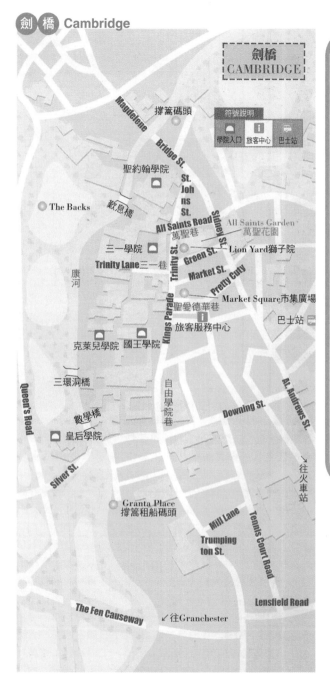

劍橋 Cambridge

劍橋 CAMBRIDGE

符號說明
學院入口　旅客中心　巴士站

撐篙碼頭

Magdelene

Bridge St.

聖約翰學院

St. Johns St.

The Backs

歎息橋

All Saints Road

Sidney St.

萬聖巷

All Saints Garden
萬聖花園

三一學院

Trinity St.

Green St.

Lion Yard獅子院

康河

Trinity Lane 三一巷

Market St.

Pretty Cury

Kings Parade

Market Square市集廣場

聖愛德華巷

旅客服務中心

巴士站

克萊兒學院　國王學院

三環洞橋

數學橋

皇后學院

Queen's Road

自由學院巷

Downing St.

Al. Andrews St.

往火車站

Silver St.

Granta Place
撐篙租船碼頭

Mill Lane

Trumping ton St.

Tennis Court Road

The Fen Causeway

往Granchester

Lensfield Road

單元三 旅行觀光

倫敦全區圖

自助旅行

搭乘電車

搭乘計程車

倫敦精華遊

懶人旅行法

倫敦地鐵圖

我想去~ I want to go (to) ~~.	~~在哪裡？ Where is the ~~?

請問到~~怎麼走？
Excuse me, can you please tell me how to go to ~~?

請告訴我現在的位置。（出示地圖）
Please tell me my current location.

劍橋大學 Cambridge University	三一學院 Trinity College
國王學院 King's College	皇后學院 Queen's College
聖約翰學院 St. John's College	克萊兒學院 Clare College
萬聖花園 All Saints Garden	布雷克威爾書店 Blackwell's Bookstore

牛 津 Oxford

| 我想去~~ | ~~在哪裡？ |
| I want to go (to) ~~. | Where is the ~~? |

請問到~~怎麼走？
Excuse me, can you please tell me how to go to ~~?

請告訴我現在的位置。（出示地圖）
Please tell me my current location.

單元三 旅行觀光

倫敦全區圖

自助旅行

搭乘電車

搭乘計程車

倫敦精華遊

懶人旅行法

倫敦地鐵圖

德漢學院

書店

新學院
New College
Hertford

萬靈學院　皇后學院

Oriel St.

Merton St.

莫德林學院

督教會學院

摩頓學院

Botanic Garden

River
Cherwell

Christ Church Meadow

Holywell Mill Stream

Queen's Lane

	瓦德漢學院 Wadham College
	基督教會學院 Christ Church College
牛津大學 Oxford University	摩頓學院 Merton College
莫德林學院 Magdalen College	卡法斯塔 Carfax Tower
基督聖體學院 Corpus Christi College	布雷克威爾書店 Blackwell's Bookstore

單元三 旅行觀光

倫敦全區圖

自助旅行

搭乘電車

搭乘計程車

倫敦精華遊

懶人旅行法

倫敦地鐵圖

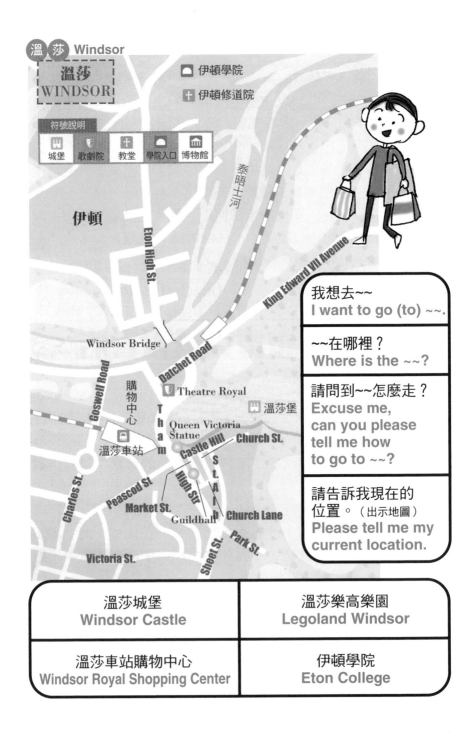

溫 莎 Windsor

溫莎
WINDSOR

伊頓學院

伊頓修道院

符號說明

城堡　歌劇院　教堂　學院入口　博物館

伊頓

泰晤士河

Eton High St.

King Edward VII Avenue

Windsor Bridge

Datchet Road

Goswell Road

購物中心

Theatre Royal

溫莎堡

Queen Victoria Statue

溫莎車站

Castle Hill

Church St.

Charles St.

Peascod St

High Str

Market St.

Guildhall

Church Lane

Park St.

Sheet St.

Victoria St.

我想去~~
I want to go (to) ~~.

~~在哪裡？
Where is the ~~?

請問到~~怎麼走？
Excuse me,
can you please
tell me how
to go to ~~?

請告訴我現在的
位置。（出示地圖）
Please tell me my
current location.

溫莎城堡 Windsor Castle	溫莎樂高樂園 Legoland Windsor
溫莎車站購物中心 Windsor Royal Shopping Center	伊頓學院 Eton College

巴 斯 Bath

皇家新月樓

服裝博物館

Brock Stree

The Circus

Bartlett St

Gay Street

George St

Broad St

Milsom St

郵政博物館

The Podium

Barton Street

Henrietta Park

Northgate

New Bond St

普特尼橋

Bridge St

Argyle St

Great Pulteney St

Upper Borough

維多利亞
藝廊

Grand Parade

High St

Cross Bath

Union St

Cheap St

巴斯修道院

Recreation
Ground

Westgate St

Westgate Bldgs

Pump Room

Bath St

York Street

莎莉露之屋

羅馬浴池博物館

Pierrepont St.

Manvers St.

巴斯
BATH

符號說明

博物館　教堂

火車站

倫敦全區圖

自助旅行

搭乘電車

搭乘計程車

倫敦精華遊

懶人旅行法

倫敦地鐵圖

羅馬浴池博館 Roman Bath Museum	皇家新月樓 Royal Crescent
巴斯修道院 Bath Abbey	莎莉露之屋 Sally Lunn's
維多利亞藝廊 Victoria Art Gallery	普特尼橋 Pulteney Bridge

倫敦全區圖

自助旅行

搭乘電車

搭乘計程車

倫敦精華遊

懶人旅行法

倫敦地鐵圖

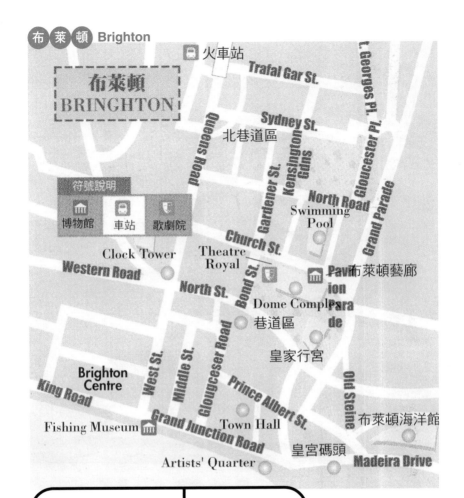

布 萊 頓 Brighton

火車站

布萊頓
BRINGHTON

符號說明

博物館　車站　歌劇院

北巷道區

Trafal Gar St.

Sydney St.

St. Georges Pl.

Gloucester Pl.

Queens Road

Gardener St.

Kensington Gdns

North Road

Grand Parade

Swimming Pool

Church St.

Clock Tower

Theatre Royal

Bond St.

Pavilion

布萊頓藝廊

Western Road

North St.

Dome Complex

Parade

巷道區

皇家行宮

West St.

Middle St.

Gloucgeser Road

Prince Albert St.

Old Steine

布萊頓海洋館

Brighton Centre

King Road

Fishing Museum

Grand Junction Road

Town Hall

皇宮碼頭

Madeira Drive

Artists' Quarter

我想去~~
I want to go (to) ~~.

~~在哪裡？
Where is the ~~?

請問到~~怎麼走？
Excuse me, can you please tell me how to go to ~~?

請告訴我現在的位置。（出示地圖）
Please tell me my current location.

巷道區
The Lanes

皇家行宮
Royal Pavilion

皇宮碼頭
Palace Pier

這裡有沒有市區觀光巴士？
Is there any city tour bus here?

有沒有一天或半天的觀光團？
Is there any one-day or half-day tour?

會去哪些地方玩？ What places will they go?	大概要花多久時間？ How long will it take?
幾點出發？ When is the departure time?	幾點回來？ When will they come back?

從哪裡出發？
Where do they set out?

→P.14

在~~飯店可以上車嗎？
Can I take on the bus in ~~ Hotel?

乘車券要在哪裡買呢？
Where can I buy the bus ticket?

→P.16

在~~飯店可以下車嗎？
May I get off at the ~~ Hotel?

可以在這裡拍照嗎？ May I take a picture here?	可以使用閃光燈嗎？ May I use the flashlight?

可以請你幫我拍照嗎？
Can you take a picture for me?

可以跟你合照嗎？
May I take a picture with you?

單元三 旅行觀光

倫敦全區圖

自助旅行

搭乘電車

搭乘計程車

倫敦精華遊

懶人旅行法

倫敦地鐵圖

單元三 旅行觀光

倫敦全區圖

自助旅行

搭乘電車

搭乘計程車

倫敦精華遊

懶人旅行法

倫敦地鐵圖

Key to lines

Bakerloo		Waterloo & City	
Central		Metropolitan	
Circle		Northern	
District		Piccadilly	
East London		Victoria	
Hammersmith & City		Docklands Light Railway	
Jubilee		British Rail	

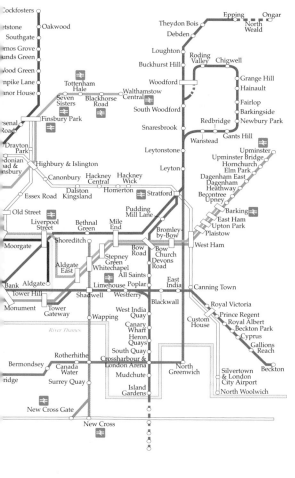

我想去~
I want to go (to) ~~.

~~在哪裡？
Where is the ~~?

請問到~~怎麼走？
Excuse me,
can you please
tell me how
to go to ~~?

請告訴我現在的位置。（出示地圖）
Please tell me my current location.

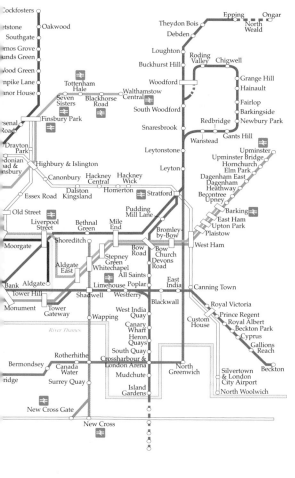

Cockfosters
etstone
Oakwood
Southgate
rnos Grove
unds Green
Wood Green
mpike Lane
anor House
Tottenham Hale
Seven Sisters
Blackhorse Road
Walthamstow Central
rsenal
Road
Finsbury Park
South Woodford
Drayton Park
Highbury & Islington
Canonbury
Hackney Central
Hackney Wick
Leytonstone
Leyton
Essex Road
Dalston Kingsland
Homerton
Stratford
Old Street
Liverpool Street
Bethnal Green
Mile End
Pudding Mill Lane
Moorgate
Shoreditch
Bow Road
Bow Church
Stepney Green
Whitechapel
Devons Road
Aldgate East
All Saints
Bank
Aldgate
Limehouse
Poplar
East India
Tower Hill
Shadwell
Westferry
Blackwall
Monument
Tower Gateway
West India Quay
Wapping
Canary Wharf
Heron Quays
Bermondsey
Rotherhithe
Canada Water
South Quay
Crossharbour & London Arena
North Greenwich
ridge
Surrey Quay
Mudchute
Island Gardens
New Cross Gate
New Cross

Epping
Ongar
Theydon Bois
North Weald
Debden
Loughton
Roding Valley
Chigwell
Buckhurst Hill
Woodford
Grange Hill
Hainault
Fairlop
Barkingside
Newbury Park
Redbridge
Snaresbrook
Gants Hill
Waristead
Upminster
Upminster Bridge
Hornchurch,
Elm Park
Dagenham East
Dagenham Heathway
Becontree
Upney
Barking
East Ham
Upton Park
Plaistow
West Ham
Canning Town
Royal Victoria
Prince Regent
Royal Albert
Custom House
Beckton Park
Cyprus
Gallions Reach
Beckton
Silvertown & London City Airport
North Woolwich

River Thames

N
W E
S

單元三 旅行觀光

倫敦全區圖

自助旅行

搭乘電車

搭乘計程車

倫敦精華遊

懶人旅行法

倫敦地鐵圖

1.英式美食

到~~吃東西吧！
Let's eat at~~.

餐廳種類	快餐店 Snack bar	啤酒屋 Beerhouse
露天咖啡座 Outdoor Cafe		餐館 Restaurant
高級餐廳 First class restaurant		大眾餐館 Public restaurant

請給我菜單 Please give me the menu.	請給我~~ I would like to have~~
請給我和那個相同的菜~~ The same order with that ~~	
請給我~~套餐。 Please give me the ~~ Meal. 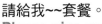	
買單！ Check, please!	多少錢？ →P.62 How much?
已經含稅及服務費了嗎？ Is tax and tips included?	可以用信用卡付費嗎？ Can I pay by credit card?

口味喜好		稍微一點點 Slightly	非常 Very
甜 Sweet	酸 Sour	鹹 Salty	苦 Bitter
辣 Hot (Spicy)	澀 Astringent	清淡 Light	油膩 Greasy
難吃 Yucky		好吃；美味 Tasty	

餐具	餐巾 Towel	筷子 Chopsticks
刀 Knife	叉 Fork	湯匙 Spoon

調味料		鹽 Salt	砂糖 Sugar
胡椒 Pepper	辣椒 Chili	番茄醬 Ketchup	醬汁 Sauce

英式美食

食材煮法

飲食種類

水果飲料

★在餐廳用餐時，小費大約占消費額的10%到15%左右。

單元四 料理飲食

英式美食
食材煮法
飲食種類
水果飲料

你喜歡~~嗎？
Do you like ~~?

我喜歡吃~~
I like to eat ~~.

食材 Materials	牛肉 Beef	豬肉 Pork	羊肉 Mutton
雞肉 Chicken	鵝肉 Goose	鴨肉 Duck	兔肉 Rabbit
火腿 Ham	臘腸 Sausage	沙拉 Salad	鮪魚 Tuna
麵類 Noodles	米飯 Rice	比目魚 Flatfish	蔬菜 Vegetable
酒燜雞肉 Chicken stew with wine		海鮮 Seafood	梭魚 Pike
鱈魚 Codfish	烏賊 Squid	龍蝦 Lobster	生蠔 Oyster

冷 Cold	熱 Hot

料理方式 Cooking	煎 Fry	炸 Deep fry	炒 Stir fry
爆 Fry	蒸 Steam	烤 Roast	煮 Boil
燴 Braise	滷 Stew	焙 Broil	燉 Stew
湯 Soup	涮 Boil	脆 Crispy	羹 Thick soup

你想吃什麼菜？
What do you like to eat?

我想吃~~
I want to have~~.

早餐 Breakfast	午餐 Lunch	晚餐 Dinner

英國料理 British Food	中華料理 Chinese Food	法國料理 French Food
義大利料理 Italian Food	印度菜 Indian Food	北非料理 North African food

菜單常用名詞 Common vocabularies on menu			開胃菜 appetizer
小菜 Side dish	湯 Soup	主菜 Entree	甜點 Dessert
佐餐酒 Wine	高湯 Broth		魚湯 Fish broth
沙拉 Salad	蜂蜜 Honey		果醬 Jam

酒類 Wines	葡萄酒 Wine	紅酒 Red wine
白酒 White wine	香檳 Champagne	雪利酒 Sherry

點心 Dessert	英式圓餅 Cookies	草莓派 Strawberry pie
蘋果派 Apple pie	白朗峰 Mont Blanc	熱巧克力 Hot Chocolate
水果糖 Fruit candy	杏桃果醬 Apricots jam	水果冰淇淋 Fruit ice cream
法國麵包 French Bread		鄉村麵包 Country style bread
千層派 Multi-layer Pie	檸檬派 Lemon pie	洋芋片 Potato chips
爆米花 Popcorn	果凍 Jelly	布丁 Pudding
蛋糕 Cake	小餅乾 Cookie	甜甜圈 Donut

水果 Fruits		
草莓 Strawberry	蘋果 Apple	
葡萄 Grape	櫻桃 Cherry	
柿子 Persimmon	橘子 Tangerine	
柳橙 Orange	梨子 Pear	
水蜜桃（桃子） Peach	番茄 Tomato	
香蕉 Banana	鳳梨 Pineapple	
哈蜜瓜（香瓜） Muskmelon	西瓜 Watermelon	
檸檬 Lemon	葡萄柚 Grapefruit	

飲料 Soft drink		鮮奶 Milk
紅茶 Black tea	咖啡 Coffee	可樂 Coke
開水 Water	熱開水 Hot water	礦泉水 Mineral water
柳丁汁 Orange juice	冰咖啡 Iced Coffee	熱咖啡 Hot coffee
奶茶 Milk tea	冰紅茶 Iced tea	熱紅茶 Hot tea

熱的 Hot	冷的 Cold

大杯 Large	中杯 Medium	小杯 Small

單元五 購物

1.主要購物中心

(1)二手貨市集

波多貝羅市集
Portobello

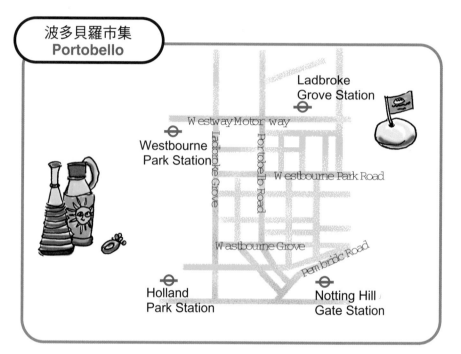

Ladbroke
Grove Station

Westway Motor way

Westbourne
Park Station

Ladbroke Grove

Portbello Road

Westbourne Park Road

Westbourne Grove

Pembric Road

Holland
Park Station

Notting Hill
Gate Station

我想去~~ **I want to go (to) ~~.**	~~在哪裡？ **Where is the ~~?**
請問到~~怎麼走？ **Excuse me, can you please tell me how to go to ~~?**	
請告訴我現在的位置。（出示地圖） **Please tell me my current location.**	

肯頓市集
Camden

肯頓運河市場
Canal Market

馬廄市場
Stables Market

肯頓水門市場
Camden Lock Market

Canal Railway

Jamestown Road

Chalk Farm Road

Kentish Town Road

Camden High Street

肯頓市場
Camden market

Inverness
Street Market

Camden Town

格林威治市集
Greenwich

National Maritime
Museum

View of Dome
Development

格林威治公園
Greenwich Park

泰晤士河
River Thames
Pier

Nelson Road

King William Walk

Village Market

Greenwich
Market

Greenwich Church St.

Weekend Market

格林威治車站

Greenwich High Rd.

襯裙巷市集
Petticoat Lane

Petticoat Lane

Aldgate East

Aldgate

單元五 購物

主要購物中心

購物逛街

衣服採購

電器禮品

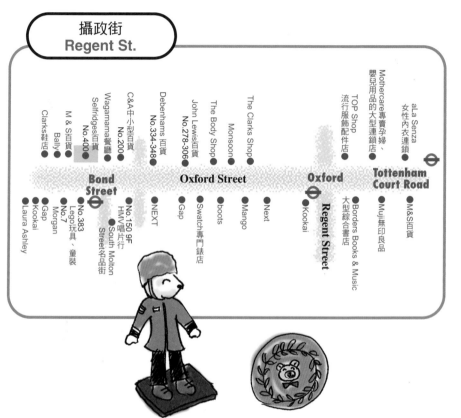

攝政街 Regent St.

Clarks鞋店
M & S百貨
Selfridges百貨 No.400
Wagamama餐廳 No.200
C&A中小型百貨 No.200
Debenhams 百貨 No.334-348
John Lewis百貨 No.278-306
The Body Shop
Monsoon
The Clarks Shop

TOP Shop 流行服飾配件店
Mothercare專賣孕婦、嬰兒用品的大型連鎖店
aLa Senza 女性內衣連鎖

Bond Street　　**Oxford Street**　　**Oxford**　　**Tottenham Court Road**

Laura Ashley
Kookai
Gap
Morgan No.7
Lego玩具、童裝 No.383
South Molton Street名品街 No.150 9F
HMV唱片行
NEXT
Gap
Swatch專門錶店
boots
Mango
Next
Kookai

Regent Street

Borders Books & Music 大型綜合書店
Muji無印良品
M&S百貨

我想去~~ I want to go (to) ~~.	~~在哪裡？ Where is the ~~?

請問到~~怎麼走？
Excuse me, can you please tell me how to go to ~~?

請告訴我現在的位置。（出示地圖）
Please tell me my current location.

查令十字路（書店街）
Charing Cross Road

Waterstone●
Foyles●

Love Joys成人書店●

●Black Wells綜合書店
●Sportpages運動書店

Charing Cross Road

●Media Z & Zwemmer
●Al Hoda
Murder One●　●Design Z設計藝術類書店
●Shipley
●Silver Moon女性書店
Comic Showcase●　●Book Bought
●The Charing Cross Road Bookshop
●Stanford Gallery

 Charing Cross Road

書店街 **Bookstore street**	成人書店 **Adult bookstore**
綜合書店 **Bookstore**	運動書店 **Sport bookstore**
設計藝術書店 **Art design bookstore**	女性書店 **Feminine bookstore**

主要購物中心

購物逛街

衣服採購

電器禮品

牛津街
Oxford St.

Tottenham
Court Road

Oxford Street

Oxford

French Connection ●

United Colors of Benetton旗艦店 ●

Godiva巧克力專賣店 ●

Crabtree Evelynee沐浴香精用品 ●

The Pen Shop名牌筆店 ●

Burberry英國傳統名牌 ●

Lego玩具及童裝 ●
Past Time複製品專門店 ●

English Teddy Bear ●
Whittard Tea禮品最佳選購處 ●

L'Odeoa下午茶好去處 ●

Regent Street

● Shellys流行鞋店
● Karen Millen總店
● Laura Asheley總店
● Bally
● Liberty自由百貨公司
● Halmely
● Levis Original總店
● NEXT 中價連鎖服飾
● Waterford Wedgewood
● Bally
● GAP Kids
● Disney Store迪士尼
● ZARA
● Austin Reed
● Aquascutum
● The Scotch House

● Burger King漢堡飽王
● Boots健康用品店
● The Body Shop

皮卡地里圓環

Piccadilly
Street

我想去~~ I want to go (to) ~~.	~~在哪裡？ Where is the ~~?
請問到~~怎麼走？ Excuse me, can you please tell me how to go to ~~?	
請告訴我現在的位置。（出示地圖） Please tell me my current location.	

騎士橋 Knightsbridge

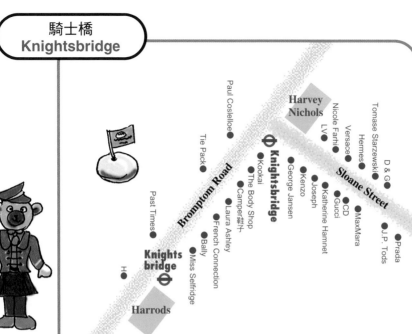

Paul Coslielloe

Harvey Nichols

Tomase Starzewski
Nicole Farhii
Hermes
Versace
LV
Gucci
CD
Kenzo
Joseph
Katherine Hamnet
George Jansen
MaxMara

D & G
J.P. Tods
Prada

Sloane Street

Tie Pack

Brompton Road

Knightsbridge
Kookai
The Body Shop
Camper 鞋子
Laura Ashley
French Connection
Bally
Miss Selfridge

Past Times

Knights bridge

Harrods

國王路 Kings Road

Cafe Rouge 連鎖咖啡店
英國設計師自營小店

Jonny Moke

Bluebird 有露天座的餐廳

Heals 居家用品店
Habitat 居家用品店

The Tratalgar Nature Pub
英國傳統酒吧

Angelic 芳香蠟燭連鎖

Nature Fact 自然風服飾店

The Whitted Tea & Coffee
知名茶店

French Connection
連鎖服飾

Nine West 連鎖服飾
OASIS 連鎖服飾
NEXT 連鎖服飾
Original Levis Shop
The Body Shop

GAP女、童裝
BALLY

Peter Jones 家居百貨

WH Smith 連鎖書店
Knicker Box 女性內衣連鎖
Whistles 綜合多種
品牌的女性服飾連鎖

Kookai 連鎖服飾

NAF NAF 連鎖服飾

La Senza 女性內衣連鎖

Monsoon Home 家居日用品店

Karen Miller
Morgan 連鎖服飾

Muji 無印良品

M & S 連鎖百貨

Joseph Sale Shop 英法品牌折扣店

Lush 生活沐浴用品店

Starbucks Coffee 連鎖咖啡店

Coffee Republic

Steiberg & Tolken
居家用品店

The Holding Company
居家用品店

包羅萬象的珠寶服飾店

Mulberry 居家用品店

Designer 居家用品店

Sloane Square

55

請給我看這個／那個～。
Please show me the / that~~.

請拿~~的給我看。
Please give me the ~~ one.

有沒有~~一點的？
Do you have a ~~ one?

我要買~~。
I want to buy ~~.

不用了。(不買)
No, thank you.

P.62

總共多少錢？
How much for all?

可以用信用卡結帳嗎？
Can I pay by credit card?

算便宜一點吧！
Make it cheaper!

可以退稅嗎？
Can I have tax refund?

這附近有沒有~~？
Is there any ~~ around here?

P.14

~~在哪裡呢？
Where is the ~~?

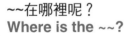

商店名稱 Store's Name		水果店 Fruit store	P.48
藥房 Pharmacy P.80		花店 Florist	
書店 Bookstore P.53		蛋糕店 Bakery P.47	
	唱片行 Record shop	點心店 Dessert shop P.47	
鞋店 Shoe shop		理髮店 (男) Barber shop	
	洗衣店 Laundry	美容院 (女) Beauty salon	
玩具店 Toy shop P.60		電器行 Appliances store P.61	
	鐘錶行 Watch store	P.61 攝影器材店 Photo equipment store	
眼鏡行 Eyeglasses store		P.80 醫院 Hospital	
P.60 文具店 Stationery		西服店 Suit store P.58	

單元五 購物

主要購物中心

購物逛街

衣服採購

電器禮品

★英國商店的營業時間最早是從上午十點到下午八點，大部分的商店星期六照常營業，而愈來愈多的店家連星期天也開門營業。

57

3.衣服採購

請給我~~ Please give me the ~~	有~~嗎? Do you have ~~?
我要這個。 I want this.	多少錢? How much? P.62
好看。 It looks good.	不好看。 It looks not so good.
我不太喜歡。 I don't like it.	

衣服 Clothes	大衣 Overcoat	外套 Coat
西裝上衣 Waistcoat	褲子 trousers	領帶 Tie
襯衫 Shirt		罩衫 Blouse
裙子 Skirt	女褲 Pants	連身裙 Jumper
套裝 Suit		毛衣 Sweater
衫 Undershirt	T恤 T-Shirt	牛仔褲 Jeans
皮衣 Leather	內衣 Underwear	泳衣 Swimsuit

配件 Accessory		手套 Gloves
帽子 Hat		短襪 Socks
長襪 Stockings		皮帶 Belt
手帕 Handkerchief		圍巾 Scarf
鞋子 Shoes		香水 Perfume

大小 Size	大 Large	小 Small	新 New
長 Long	短 Short	厚 Thick	薄 Thin

顏色 Color		黑色 Black
藍色 Blue	白色 White	紅色 Red
黃色 Yellow	綠色 Green	橘色 Orange
灰色 Gray	紫色 Purple	粉紅色 Pink

4.電器禮品

單元五 購物
主要購物中心
購物逛街
衣服採購
電器禮品

歡迎光臨 Welcome!
哪裡有賣~~ Where can I find the ~~?
有~~嗎? Do you have~~?
我可以試試看嗎? Can I try it?
有打折嗎? Do you have a discount?

~~折扣 ~~% off | 要/不要 Yes / No | 賣完了 Sold out

買一送一 Buy one get one free | 貴/便宜 Expensive / Cheap

退貨 Return | 收銀台 Cashier

說明書 Manual | 保證書 Guarantee certificate

禮品文具 Stationery | 記事簿 Datebook | 筆記本 Notebook | 原子筆 pen

信封 Envelop | 明信片 Postcard | 便利貼 Post-it | 包裝紙 Wrapping

60

電器、日用品 **Appliances**	電視 **Television**
音響 **Audio**	手機 **Cellular phone**
數位相機 **Digital camera**	電話 **Telephone**
刮鬍刀 **Razor**	隨身聽 **Walkman**
CD隨身聽 **CD walkman**	相機 **Camera**
錄影機 **Video recorder**	電腦 **Computer**
時鐘 **Clock**	手錶 **Watch**

主要購物中心

購物逛街

衣服採購

電器禮品

1.數字金錢

誰？ Who?	哪裡？ Where?	什麼？ What?	為什麼？ Why?
幾點鐘？ What time?		多少錢？ How much?	哪個？ Which?
有~~嗎？ Do you have ~~?		我在找~~ I am looking for ~~	問誰好呢？ Whom should I ask?

數字	1 One	2 Two	3 Three
4 Four	5 Five	6 Six	7 Seven
8 Eight	9 Nine	10 Ten	11 Eleven
12 Twelve	13 Thirteen	14 Fourteen	15 Fifteen
16 Sixteen	17 Seventeen	18 Eighteen	19 Nineteen
20 Twenty	30 Thirty	40 Forty	50 Fifty
60 Sixty	70 Seventy	80 Eighty	90 Ninety
100 A hundred	500 Five hundreds	1000 A thousand	10000 Ten thousands

現金 Cash 	信用卡 Credit card	旅行支票 Traveler's check

零錢 Change	英鎊 Pound	歐元 EURO	美金 Dollar	台幣 NT dollar

個 piece	號 size	杯 cup
位 person	件 piece	包 pack

天 Day	個月 Month	年 Year	時 Hour

公里 Kilometer	公尺 Millimeter	公分 Centimeter

公斤 Kilogram	公克 gram	公升 Liter	毫升 cc.

★在英國使用的貨幣是以鎊為單位，1鎊等於100便士（P），而信用卡在英國倫敦的使用相當普遍，很容易就可以找到能夠使用的銀行和商店。

今天是幾月幾日星期幾?
What date is today?

幾月？
What month?

一月 **January**	二月 **February**	三月 **March**	四月 **April**
五月 **May**	六月 **June**	七月 **July**	八月 **August**
九月 **September**	十月 **October**	十一月 **November**	十二月 **December**

幾日(號)？
What date is today?

星期幾？
What day is today?

星期日 **Sunday**	星期一 **Monday**	星期二 **Tuesday**	星期三 **Wednesday**
星期四 **Thursday**	星期五 **Friday**	星期六 **Saturday**	

春 Spring	夏 Summer 
秋 Autumn	冬 Winter

氣候 Weather	熱 Hot	冷 Cold
涼爽 Cool	舒適 Cosy	溫暖 Warm

新年
New year

★英國是溫帶海洋氣候，屬於潮溼而溫和的國家，在這裡夏季的平均溫度為攝氏15~20度，冬天則為5~7度。再加上英國的緯度較高，所以到了夏季即使是八、九點天色仍很明亮，不過一旦到了冬天，大約下午四點太陽就下山了。

3.時間標示

數字金錢

年月季節

時間標示

現在幾點鐘？ **What time is it?**	幾點鐘出發？ **When do we departure?**
幾點鐘到達？ **When will we arrive?**	要花多久時間？ **How long will it take?**
請在~~點叫我起床。 **Please wake me up at ~~.**	
在~~見面吧！ **Let's meet at ~~.**	沒時間！ **I have no time.**
趕時間！ **I am in a hurry.**	快點！ **Hurry up.**

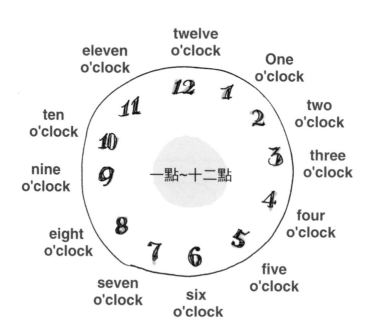

一點~十二點

twelve o'clock
eleven o'clock
One o'clock
ten o'clock
two o'clock
nine o'clock
three o'clock
eight o'clock
four o'clock
seven o'clock
five o'clock
six o'clock

66

幾分？	1分鐘 one minute	2分鐘 two minutes	3分鐘 three minutes
4分鐘 four minutes	5分鐘 five minutes	6分鐘 six minutes	7分鐘 seven minutes
8分鐘 eight minutes	9分鐘 nine minutes	10分鐘 ten minutes	11分鐘 eleven minutes

12分鐘 twelve minutes	13分鐘 thirteen minutes	14分鐘 fourteen minutes
15分鐘 fifteen minutes	16分鐘 sixteen minutes	17分鐘 seventeen minutes
18分鐘 eighteen minutes	19分鐘 nineteen minutes	20分鐘 twenty minutes
21分鐘 twenty-one minutes	22分鐘 twenty-two minutes	23分鐘 twenty-three minutes
30分鐘 thirty minutes	40分鐘 forty minutes	50分鐘 fifty minutes

聖誕節 Christmas	萬聖節 Halloween	復活節 Easter	勞動節 May Day

蘇格蘭銀行休日 Scotland bank holiday	八月銀行休假日 August bank holiday

春季銀行休假日 Spring bank holiday	藝穗節 Fringe	愛丁堡藝術節 Edinburgh Festival

國際藝術節 International Festival	愛丁堡書展 Edinburgh Book Festival

★冬令時間時，倫敦比台北晚八個小時，而夏令時間則為晚七個小時。

單元七 文化生活

1.休閒文化

你喜歡~~? Do you like~~?	喜歡 Yes.	不喜歡 No.	普通 So so.

你知道~~嗎 Do you know~~?	知道 Yes.	不知道 No.

我喜歡~~ I like ~~	~~受歡迎嗎？ Is ~~ popular here?

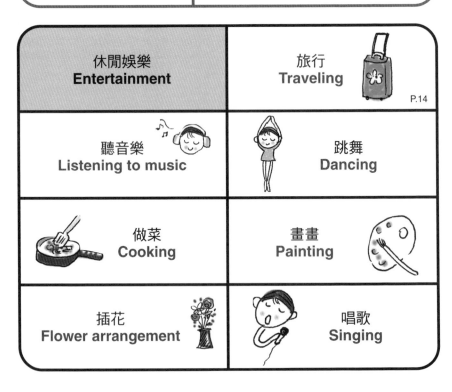

休閒娛樂 Entertainment	旅行 Traveling P.14
聽音樂 Listening to music	跳舞 Dancing
做菜 Cooking	畫畫 Painting
插花 Flower arrangement	唱歌 Singing

運動 **Sport**	游泳 **Swimming**
登山 **Climbing**	健行 **Hiking**
網球 **Tennis**	足球 **Football**

名人 **Celebrity**		女王伊莉莎白二世 **Queen Elizabeth II**
愛丁堡公爵菲利浦 **Prince Philip, Duke of Edinburgh**		蘇菲 **Sophie, Countess of Wessex**
愛德華王子 **Prince Edward, Earl of Wessex**		莎拉 **Sarah, Duchess of York**
安德魯王子 **Prince Andrew, Duke of York**		貝克漢 **David Backham**
皇家公主安娜 **Princess Anna**	黛安娜王妃 **Princess Diana**	查理斯王子 **Charles, Prince of Wales**

2.藝術時尚

你知道~~嗎 Do you know~~?	知道 Yes.	不知道 No.

我喜歡~~
I like ~~

文學 Literature		莎士比亞 Shakespeare	
羅密歐與茱麗葉 Romeo and Juliet		哈姆雷特 Hamlet	
馬克白 Macbeth	亨利五世 Henry V	珍奧斯丁 Jane Austin	
狄更生 Charles Dickens		布朗蒂姐妹 Bronte Sisters	
布雷克 William Blake		濟慈 John Keats	

藝術 **Art**	音樂家 **Musician**
古典音樂 **Classics (Classical music)**	
歌劇 **Opera**	指揮 **Conductor**
作曲家 **Composer**	建築藝術 **Art of Architecture**
藝術家 **Artist**	劇場 **Theatre**
劇場工作者 **Theatre worker**	電影 **Film**
男演員 **Actor**	女演員 **Actress**
導演 **Director**	編劇 **Playwright**

2.藝術時尚

你喜歡~~? Do you like~~?	喜歡 Yes.	不喜歡 No.

流行時尚 Fashion	熱門音樂 Pop Music
披頭四 The Beatles	滾石合唱團 The Rolling stone
搖滾樂 Rock'n' Roll	艾爾頓強 Elton John
大衛鮑伊 David Bowe	U2合唱團 U2

酒館文化 Pub and Bar	啤酒 Beer
淡啤酒 Lager	苦啤酒 Bitter
褐麥啤酒 Ale	愛爾蘭黑麥啤酒 Gunnies

威士忌 Whisky	葡萄酒 Wine	雞尾酒 Cocktail

單元八 介紹問候

1.自我介紹

單元八 介紹問候

自我介紹

嗜好星座

朋友關係

約會確認

基本資料 **Personal information**	我叫~~ **My name is ~~**
可以告訴我你的姓名嗎？ **May I have your name?**	
我是台灣人 **I am Taiwanese.**	
你去過台灣嗎？ **Have you ever been to Taiwan before?**	

我的職業是~~ **My occupation is ~~**		老師 **Teacher**
學生 **Student**	公務員 **Public servant**	上班族 **Employee**
家庭主婦 **Housewife**	律師 **Lawyer**	銀行職員 **Bank clerk**
秘書 **Secretary**	作家 **Writer**	醫生 **Doctor**
記者 **Reporter**	公司老闆 **Employer**	沒有工作 **unemployed**

我的嗜好是~~ My hobby is (are) ~~		網球 Tennis
棒球 Baseball	旅行 Traveling	看電影 Watching movies
游泳 Swimming	登山 Climbing	健行 Hiking
聽音樂 Listening to music	跳舞 Dancing	做菜 Cooking
畫畫 Painting	插花 Flower arrangement	唱歌 Singing
家人 Family	父親 Father	母親 Mother
祖父母 Grandparents	小孩 Child	兒子 Son
女兒 Daughter	丈夫 Husband	妻子 Wife

我的星座是~~
My constellation is ~~

	牡羊座 **Aries**		金牛座 **Taurus**
雙子座 **Gemini**		巨蟹座 **Cancer**	
	獅子座 **Leo**		處女座 **Virgo**
天秤座 **Libra**		天蠍座 **Scorpio**	
	射手座 **Sagittarius**		魔羯座 **Capricorn**
水瓶座 **Aquarius**		雙魚座 **Pisces**	

有 	是	不是
Yes	Yes	No

這位	那位
This	That

我	你	他	她
I	You	He	She

我們	他們／她們
We	They

愛上	相愛	談戀愛
In love with	Love each other	Fall in love

結婚	離婚
Marry	Divorce

婚外情	分手
Affair	Breakup

單元八 介紹問候

自我介紹

嗜好星座

朋友關係

約會確認

~~是我最要好的朋友。
~~ is my best friend.

約會 Date	有默契 Tacit understanding
談得來 Get along with	吵架 Have a fight
室友 Roommate	男朋友 Boy friend
情婦 Mistress	女朋友 Girl friend
朋友 Friend	好朋友 Good friend
同居人 The one I live with	鄰居 Neighbor
附近 Nearby	鄉下 Countryside 

4.約會確認

哈囉 Hello	你好嗎？ How do you do?	好久不見 Long time no see.

一切都好嗎？ How's everything going?	何時見面？ When shall we meet? P.66

我們要約在哪裡？ Where shall we meet?	我能去。 I can make it.

我不能去。 I can't make it.	我想和你一起去! I want to go with you.

請來接我一起去!
Please come and pick me up.

告訴我你的行動電話號碼。
Please tell my your cellular phone number.

我會再打給你。 I will call you again.	請打電話給我。 Please call me.

NOTE

要搭什麼時候的巴士？
What's the time of our bus?　P.16、66

要坐什麼時候的電車？
What's the time of our train?　P.16、66

什麼時候到達？
When will we arrive?　P.66

要花多久時間？
How long will it take?　P.66

幾個小時？
How many hours will it take?　P.66

多少分鐘？
How many minutes will it take?　P.66

我很抱歉。 **I am sorry.**	我沒辦法答應。 **I can't promise you.**	時間 **Time**	地點 **Place**

我太忙了,沒辦法答應。
I am too busy to make it.

我迷路了。 **I am lost.**	我遺失了你的電話號碼。 **I lost your phone number.**

我遲到了。 **I am late.**	我找不到地方。 **I can't find the Place.**

原諒我。 **Forgive me.**	我需要幫忙。 **I need help.**	我現在在哪裡？ **Where am I now?**

國際電話怎麼打？
How to make an international call?

★台灣打電話到英國為002-44-區域碼(去0)-電話號碼；而從英國打電話到台灣則為00-886-區域號碼(去0)-電話號碼,從西元二千年四月起,原倫敦的0171區碼改為0207,而0181則改為0208。

藥品急救
Pharmacy and Emergency

請問附近有醫院嗎？
Is there any hospital around here?

請帶我去醫院。
Please take me to the hospital.

請叫救護車。
Please call the ambulance.

你吃藥了嗎？→吃了／還沒
Did you take the medicine yet? Yes / No.

請幫我買~~藥。
Please buy the ~~ for me.

不舒服 **Feel sick**	沒有食慾 **Anorectic**	喉嚨痛 **Sore throat**
咳嗽 **Cough**	拉肚子 **Diarrhea**	全身無力 **Feel weak**
嘔吐 **Puke**	發燒 **Fever**	流鼻水 **Running nose**
牙痛 **Toothache**	痛 **Ache**	劇痛 **Lancinating**

骨折 Fracture	發麻 Numb	扭傷 Sprain

頭 Head	頭髮 Hair	眉毛 Eyebrows

耳朵 Ear	牙齒 Tooth	舌頭 Tongue	肩膀 Shoulder
胸 Chest	乳房 Breasts	背 Back	肚子 Abdomen

屁股 Bottom			肛門 Anus
生殖器 Genitals			肌肉 Muscle
皮膚 Skin			指甲 Fingernail
眼睛 Eye			骨頭 Bone

鼻子 Nose	嘴巴 Mouth	脖子 Neck	手臂 Arm
手 Hand	手指 Finger	手肘 Elbow	肚臍 Bellybutton

大腿 Thigh	膝蓋 Knee	小腿 Leg
腳 Foot	腳趾 Toe	腳底 Sole

每天 Every day.	隔一天 Every other day.	每天二次 Twice a day.
每天三次 Three times a day.		每天四次 Four times a day.
食前 Before meal.		食後 After meal.
就寢前 Before sleep.		外用 External use.

有會講中文的醫生嗎?
Is there any doctor who can speak Chinese?

可以使用海外保險嗎?
Do you accept overseas insurance?

請給我診斷書。
Please give me a diagnosis paper.

多長時間能治好。
How long will it take for me to get well?

這個藥會不會引起副作用？
Is there any side effect of the drug?

請保重。
Please take care.

我的血型是~~型 My blood type is ~~.	A A	B B	O O	AB AB

一天吃~~次 ~~ times a day.		頭痛藥 Headache tablets
感冒藥 Medicine for colds	止痛藥 Painkiller	鎮靜劑 Sedative
腸胃藥 Peptic	止瀉藥 Obstipantia	維生素C Vitamin C
阿司匹靈藥片 Aspirin	安眠藥 Sleeping pills	漱口劑 Mouthwash
點眼藥 Eyedrops	體溫計 Thermometer	OK繃 Band-Aids

NOTE

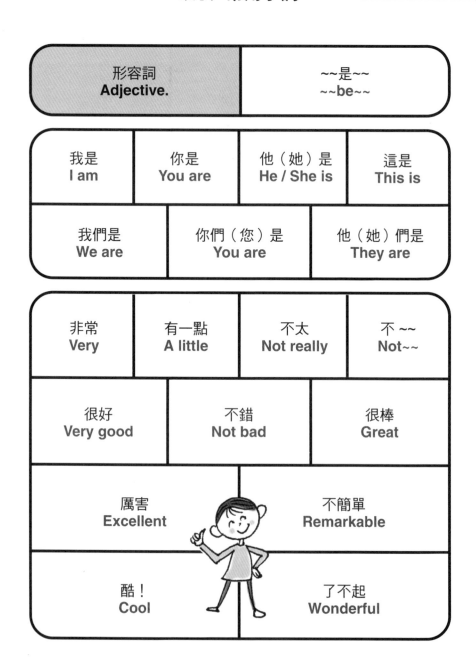

形容詞 Adjective.	~~是~~ ~~be~~

我是 I am	你是 You are	他（她）是 He / She is	這是 This is

我們是 We are	你們（您）是 You are	他（她）們是 They are

非常 Very	有一點 A little	不太 Not really	不 ~~ Not~~

很好 Very good	不錯 Not bad	很棒 Great

厲害 Excellent	不簡單 Remarkable

酷！ Cool	了不起 Wonderful

大／小 Big / Small	多／少 Many / Few	貴／便宜 Expensive / Cheap
重／輕 Heavy / Light	強／弱 Strong / Weak	新／舊 New / Old
容易／困難 Easy / Hard	好／不好 Good /Bad	長／短 Long / Short

遠／近 Far / Near	硬／軟 Hard / Soft	胖／瘦 Fat / Slim	老／年輕 Old / Young

忙碌／空閒 Busy / Free	(天氣)熱的 Hot	（天氣）冷的 Cold
潮溼的 Humid	溫暖的 Warm	涼爽的 Cool

厚的 Thick	薄的 Thin	濃的 Dense
寬廣的 Wide	狹窄的 Narrow	早的 Early
晚的；慢的 Late/Slow	快的 Fast	圓形的 Round
明亮的 Bright	黑暗的 Dark	四方形的 Square
強壯的 Strong	脆弱的 Fragile	高的；貴的 High/Expensive
矮的 Short	便宜的 Cheap	淺的 Shallow
粗的 Thick	細的 Thin	很棒 Great

新的 New	舊的 Old	大的 Big	小的 Small

簡單的 **Easy**	困難的 **Difficult**	

有趣的 **Interesting**	無聊的 **Boring**	有名（的） **Famous**
熱鬧（的） **Bustling**	安靜（的） **Quiet**	認真 **Serious**
有精神，活潑 **Vivid**	方便 **Convenient**	不方便 **Inconvenient**
漂亮（美麗） **Beautiful**	熱心（親切） **Enthusiastic**	擅長（拿手） **Good at**
不擅 **Not good at**	喜歡 **Like**	討厭 **Hate**

動詞／疑問詞
Verb/Interrogative

什麼 What	為什麼 Why	哪一個 Which	什麼時候 When
誰 Who	在哪裡 Where	怎麼 How	怎麼辦 What to do

比如說 For example	剛才 Just	現在 Now	以後 Later
想 Want to	會 Can	可以 May	比較好 Better
不想 Don't want to	不會 Can't		不能 May not

不要~比較好 would better not …
已經~了 Have(has) already
有~過 Have(has) ~~

是~ **Yes**	不是~ **Not**	還沒~ **Not yet**
沒有 **Not**	應該 **Should**	真的 **Did**

見面 **Meet**	分開 **Apart**	問 **Ask**	回答 **Answer**
教 **Teach**	學習 **Learn**	記得 **Remember**	忘記 **Forget**
進去 **Enter**	出去 **Go Out**	開始 **Start**	結束 **End**
走 **Walk**	跑 **Run**	前進 **Proceed**	找 **Look for**

停止 Stop	住 Live	回去 Go back
來 Come	哭 Cry	笑 Laugh
送 Send	接受 Accept	看書 Read
看 Watch	寫 Write	說 Talk
聽 Hear	了解 Understand	說明 Explain
知道 Know	想 Think	小心 Caution

睡覺 Sleep	起床 Wake up	休息 Rest
打開 Open	關 Close	變成 Become
做 Do	賣 Sell	故障 Break down

有 Have	沒有 Don't have	站 Stand	坐 Sit

蹲 Squat	買 Buy	使用 Use
工作 Work	喜歡 Like	討厭 Hate

附錄
Appendix

聯絡方式
Contact information

我住在 .... 飯店。
I live in the .... Hotel.

地址是 ....
The address is ....

請告訴我你的~~
Please tell me your~~

姓名 name	
地址 address	
電話號碼 phone number	
電子郵件地址 E-mail	

我會寄~~給你。 I will send a ~~ to you.	信 Letter	照片 Picture

請寫在這裡。 Please write down here.	

旅行攜帶物品備忘錄

		出發前	旅行中	回國時
重要度 A	護照（要影印）			
	簽證（有的國家不要）			
	飛機票（要影印）			
	現金（零錢也須準備）			
	信用卡			
	旅行支票			
	預防接種證明（有的國家不用）			
重要度 B	交通工具、旅館等的預約券			
	國際駕照（要影印）			
	海外旅行傷害保險證（要影印）			
	相片2張（萬一護照遺失時申請補發之用）			
	換穿衣物（以耐髒、易洗、快乾為主）			
	相機、底片、電池			
	預備錢包（請另外收藏）			
	計算機			
	地圖、時刻表、導遊書			
	辭典、會話書籍（別忘了帶這本書！）			
重要度 C	變壓器			
	筆記用具、筆記本等			
	常備醫藥、生理用品			
	裁縫用具			
	萬能工具刀			
	盥洗用具（洗臉、洗澡用具）			
	吹風機			
	紙袋、釘書機、橡皮筋			
	洗衣粉、晾衣夾			
	雨具			
	太陽眼鏡、帽子			
	隨身聽、小型收音機（可收聽當地資訊）			
	塑膠袋			

國家圖書館出版品預行編目資料

手指英國 / 不勉強工作室著 --初版. --臺北市：商周出版：城邦文化發行，2002 [民91]
面； 公分. --（旅行手指外文會話書 5）

ISBN 957-469-972-2（平裝）

1. 觀光德語 – 會話

805.188 91001608

手指英國

作　　　者／不勉強工作室
譯　　　者／林士皓
總　編　輯／林宏濤
責　任　編　輯／黃淑貞、陳玳妮

發　行　人／何飛鵬
法　律　顧　問／中天國際法律事務所周奇杉律師
出　　　版／城邦文化事業股份有限公司　商周出版
　　　　　　104台北市民生東路二段141號9樓
　　　　　　電話：(02) 25007008　傳眞：(02) 25007759
　　　　　　e-mail:bwp.service@cite.com.tw
發　　　行／英屬蓋曼群島商家庭傳媒股份有限公司城邦分公司
聯　絡　地　址／104台北市民生東路二段141號2樓
　　　　　　讀者服務專線：0800-020-299
　　　　　　24小時傳眞服務：02-2517-0999
　　　　　　劃撥：1896600-4
　　　　　　戶名：英屬蓋曼群島商家庭傳媒股份有限公司城邦分公司
　　　　　　讀者服務信箱E-mail：cs@cite.com.tw
香港發行所／城邦（香港）出版集團
　　　　　　香港灣仔駱克道193號東超商業中心1樓
　　　　　　電話：25086231　傳眞：25789337
馬新發行所／城邦（馬新）出版集團　Cite (M) Sdn. Bhd. (458372 U)
　　　　　　41, Jalan Radin Anum, Bandar Baru Sri Petaling,
　　　　　　57000 Kuala Lumpur, Malaysia. email：cite@cite.com.my
　　　　　　電話：603-90578822　傳眞：603-90576622

封　面　設　計／斐類設計
內　文　設　計／紀健龍+王亞棻
打　字　排　版／極翔企業有限公司
印　　　刷／韋懋印刷事業股份有限公司
總　經　銷／高見文化行銷股份有限公司　電話：(02)2668-9005
　　　　　　傳眞：(02)2668-9790　客服專線：0800-055-365

□ 2002年3月15日初版　　　　　　　　　　　　Printed in Taiwan.
□ 2015年5月5日二版6.5刷

售價／99元